J Furlin
Furlington, Patty,
Flower girl power /
$4.99   on1018078926

Happy Princess

Flower Girl Power

DISCARD

by Patty Furlington

Scholastic Inc.

With special thanks to Anne Marie Ryan

If you purchased this book without a cover, you should be aware that this book is stolen property. It was reported as "unsold and destroyed" to the publisher, and neither the author nor the publisher has received any payment for this "stripped book."

Text copyright © 2018 by Hothouse Fiction
Cover and interior art copyright © 2018 Scholastic Inc.

All rights reserved. Published by Scholastic Inc., *Publishers since 1920*, 557 Broadway, New York, NY 10012, by arrangement with Hothouse Fiction. Series created by Hothouse Fiction. SCHOLASTIC and associated logos are trademarks and/or registered trademarks of Scholastic Inc. PUPPY PRINCESS is a trademark of Hothouse Fiction.

The publisher does not have any control over and does not assume any responsibility for author or third-party websites or their content.

No part of this publication may be reproduced, stored in a retrieval system, or transmitted in any form or by any means, electronic, mechanical, photocopying, recording, or otherwise, without written permission of the publisher. For information regarding permission, write to Hothouse Fiction, The Old Truman Brewery, 91 Brick Lane, London E1 6QL, UK.

This book is a work of fiction. Names, characters, places, and incidents are either the product of the author's imagination or are used fictitiously, and any resemblance to actual persons, living or dead, business establishments, events, or locales is entirely coincidental.

ISBN 978-1-338-13434-6

10 9 8 7 6 5 4 3 2 1   18 19 20 21 22

Printed in the U.S.A.   40
First printing 2018

Book design by Baily Crawford

Table of Contents

Petrovia Royal Family

Rosie

Queen Fifi

King Charles

Rocky & Rollo

Chapter 1

Wedding Bells

"Are we nearly there yet?" Princess Rosie asked her mother eagerly. The small white puppy's curly ears streamed out behind her as she stuck her head out of the royal carriage. Pulled by a Shetland pony named Chester and decorated with the royal pawprint symbol, the carriage was taking Rosie and her family from Pawstone Palace to the house of her cousin Dotty.

"It's not much farther," said Rosie's mother, Queen Fifi. The elegant white Maltese straightened her diamond tiara. It matched her sparkling collar perfectly.

"Why are you so excited?" grumbled Rosie's younger brother Rocky. "I hate visiting Hound Hall."

"Yeah, why can't we stay home?" whined Rollo. Rosie's twin brothers had curly white fur like her, but Rollo had a black splotch over one eye, so it was easy to tell them apart.

"The Duke and Duchess of Dalmatia are your aunt and uncle. They're looking forward to seeing you," said Queen Fifi.

"But Aunt Coco is horrible," complained Rocky.

"She's even stricter than you," moaned Rollo.

King Charles, a portly white Maltese, chuckled. He quickly stifled his laughter with his paw when the queen glared at him.

"I expect you children to be on your best behavior while we are visiting Hound Hall," said Queen Fifi sternly. "I don't want any incidents like last time."

The last time the royal family had visited Hound Hall, the puppy princes had dug holes in the flower beds, shown up to dinner with mud on their whiskers, and smashed an antique vase during a lively game of tag.

"Don't worry, my dear," said King Charles, patting Queen Fifi with a large velvety paw. "I'm sure the princes will be as good as gold."

Rosie doubted her brothers would be able to stay out of mischief for two minutes, let alone two days! It didn't take much to upset Duchess Coco, who was very formal. But her daughter, Lady Dotty, was Rosie's favorite cousin. Kind and fun-loving, Dotty was like the big sister Rosie had always wished for. Rosie couldn't wait to see her!

"We're here!" cried Rosie as a mansion came into view.

Chester trotted up the path, his hooves clip-clopping on the cobblestones. "Hound Hall, Your Majesties," he announced, coming to a halt in front of the grand house.

"Thank you, Chester," said King Charles, slowly easing himself out of the carriage. The rest of the family climbed out after him.

"Welcome!" said Duchess Coco, walking out to greet them. She had white fur like Queen Fifi, but hers was fluffy rather than curly. The two Maltese exchanged air kisses on either side of their muzzles. "The puppies have grown so much!" exclaimed the duchess. Rosie obediently let her aunt plant a kiss on her nose, but Rocky and Rollo ducked to avoid the duchess's kisses.

A white dog with black spots bounded across the lawn. "Hello, old chap," said the Duke of Dalmatia, who was wearing sweatbands around his paws. "I was just about to go for a run. Care to join me?" he asked King Charles.

"Our journey was very tiring, so I'd better have a nap," King Charles said, yawning. "Another time, maybe."

Rocky and Rollo giggled. King Charles's going on a run with their energetic uncle was about as likely as his refusing second helpings of dessert!

"Dotty!" barked Rosie, her tail wagging wildly. She ran to her cousin and they nuzzled each other's noses affectionately.

"It's so good to see you, Rosie," said Dotty, who had fluffy hair like her mother and spots like her father. "There's someone I'd like you to meet." She beckoned to a handsome brown-and-white terrier. "This is my friend Jack Russell."

"Nice to meet you, Princess Rosie," said Jack, bowing to her. "Dotty has told me so much about you."

"What's she told you about us?" Rocky asked impishly.

"She told me that you two are royal terrors," teased Jack. "And that you love to play ball. Want to play catch in the garden?"

"Yippee!" Rocky and Rollo cried together. Yelping with excitement, the puppy princes ran off with Jack.

Rosie and her cousin went up to Dotty's bedroom. It was exactly how Rosie wanted her bedroom to look when she was older.

The walls were painted hot pink, and the bed had a cool black-and-white polka-dot bedspread. Twinkling lights shaped like cute little bones hung along the wall, and Dotty's dressing table was covered with perfume bottles and brushes. A photo of Jack and Dotty in a heart-shaped frame stood on the bedside table.

"So what's up?" Dotty asked.

"I've been really busy," Rosie told her cousin. She pushed a magazine with a picture of a bride on the cover off a fluffy pink beanbag and flopped down on the seat. "I helped organize the Royal Talent Show this year. My friend Cleo and I danced with Bella Fierce!"

"Wow!" said Dotty, impressed.

Petrovia's biggest pop star had judged the talent show and had even stayed at the palace for a few days. She and Rosie had become good friends.

"It was amazing," said Rosie.

"I love her song 'True Love,'" said Dotty. "It would be a really good song to dance to at a wedding," she added dreamily.

Rosie nodded. Bella's music was fun to dance to anytime, anywhere!

Loud barks of excitement came from outside, so Rosie went to the window to see what was going on. In the garden below, Jack was playing catch with Rocky and Rollo.

"Jack seems really nice," said Rosie.

"Yes," said Dotty. "He's very special."

A bell tinkled downstairs.

"We'd better not be late for tea," said Dotty.

Rosie and Dotty joined their parents in an elegant parlor. There were lace doilies on every surface, and on the table was a fancy china tea set. King Charles was eyeing a silver platter of cookies greedily.

"We're here!" cried Rocky, bursting into the room. Rollo tumbled in next, panting noisily before grabbing a cookie.

"Oh no!" gasped Duchess Coco, horrified. "Look at the carpet!"

The princes had tracked muddy paw prints all over the rug!

"I'll get that cleaned up," said Jack. He quickly brushed away the dirt. "The princes just didn't want to be late," he explained.

"Thanks, Jack," said Dotty.

"Did you boys have fun?" King Charles asked, helping himself to several cookies.

"It was great," said Rollo, spraying crumbs everywhere.

"Visiting here isn't going to be totally boring for once," said Rocky through a mouthful of cookie.

Duchess Coco spluttered on her tea.

"I'm sure the boys don't mean that," Queen Fifi interjected hastily.

"Sorry," said Rocky. "I just meant that Jack is awesome."

"We think so, too," said the duke.

"Actually," said Duchess Coco, "Dotty and Jack have some news . . ."

Jack went to sit by Dotty, putting one of his paws on top of hers. Dotty looked up at him adoringly.

Rosie suddenly remembered the bridal magazine, the photograph on Dotty's bedside

table, and what her cousin had said about dancing at a wedding. Everything suddenly fell into place. How had she not figured it out earlier? "You're getting married!" she blurted out.

Duchess Coco looked annoyed that Rosie had interrupted her big announcement, but Dotty and Jack nodded happily.

"Congratulations!" shouted Rosie, hugging her cousin.

Rocky and Rollo gave Jack high fives with their paws.

"When is the wedding going to be?" asked Queen Fifi.

"Soon, hopefully," said Dotty. "Once we've chosen somewhere to have it."

"Not too soon. I need to learn how to dance first," joked Jack.

"Why don't you get married at Pawstone Palace?" offered King Charles.

"Really?" asked Dotty.

"Of course," said Queen Fifi. "We'd be honored to host our niece's wedding."

"That's so kind of you," said Jack.

"Actually, we have another favor to ask," said Dotty. Turning to her cousin, she popped the question. "Rosie, would you be my bridesmaid?"

"Yes!" Rosie barked happily.

Chapter 2

The Duchess's Demands

As soon as she got back home, Rosie filled her lady-in-waiting in on the news. "Oh, Cleo, it's so romantic," Rosie said, sighing. "There's going to be a wedding at Pawstone Palace!"

"Ooh! I love weddings," Cleo said, her blue eyes shining with excitement.

"Good," said Rosie, "because you're invited."

Cleo wasn't just Rosie's lady-in-waiting; the fluffy white kitten was also her very best friend. "What does a bridesmaid do?" Cleo asked.

"I need to help the bride plan her wedding, and I will walk down the aisle holding flowers," said Rosie. "Oh, and I need to organize her bridal shower." She gulped. Being a bridesmaid was a big responsibility, and she didn't want to let Dotty down!

"Maybe we could practice," suggested Cleo.

"That's a great idea!" yelped Rosie, her tail wagging. "Let's have a pretend wedding!"

Rosie ran to the laundry room, where guinea pig maids were folding sheets under the watchful eye of Priscilla, a gray rabbit in a starched white apron.

"Make those corners crisp," Priscilla instructed the maids.

"Just borrowing this," said Rosie, grabbing a white sheet.

Priscilla tutted loudly as Rosie ran back to her bedroom. "Princesses should NEVER run," the rabbit called after her. "They should ALWAYS walk." For about the millionth time, Rosie thanked her lucky stars that Priscilla had been promoted to chief housekeeper and was no longer her lady-in-waiting. Cleo was MUCH more fun!

Back in her bedroom, Rosie draped the sheet over Cleo's head. "There," said Rosie.

"You be the bride and I'll be the bridesmaid. What are we missing?"

"Flowers?" asked Cleo.

Rosie took a bouquet of tulips out of a nearby vase and thrust them into Cleo's paws. "Is that everything?"

"Um, we need a groom and someone to marry us," said Cleo.

Rocky and Rollo bounded down the hallway, Rocky nipping playfully at his brother's tail. *They'll do*, thought Rosie.

Spreading out her paws, Rosie blocked their way. "Stop!" she cried. "We're having a wedding. We need a groom and a minister."

"Ew," said Rocky. "Weddings are silly."

"I'm never getting married," said Rollo, wrinkling his nose in disgust.

"Me neither," agreed Rocky.

Before Rosie could persuade her brothers, Theodore, the palace's long-serving tortoise butler, announced, "The Duchess of Dalmatia, Lady Dotty, and her fiancé have arrived!"

"Dotty's here!" Rosie cried. "Come on, Cleo—I want you to meet Jack." Cleo tugged off the white sheet and followed Rosie downstairs.

Queen Fifi and the guests were in the throne room, making wedding plans.

"Congratulations," Cleo told the happy couple.

"I saw you in the Royal Talent Show," said Jack. "I wish I could dance like you—I've got four left paws."

"You could have the wedding in here," suggested Queen Fifi. The throne room had beautiful wood-paneled walls and colorful banners. Rosie thought Dotty and Jack would look elegant sitting on the king's and queen's gold thrones.

"I'm not sure it's quite right," said Duchess Coco.

They went outside, into the palace's beautiful gardens.

"We could set up a big tent in the garden," offered Queen Fifi.

"That sounds wonderful!" Dotty said.

Duchess Coco shuddered. "Too dirty," she said.

They trooped back inside. "How about the ballroom?" Queen Fifi suggested.

Duchess Coco gazed around at the room's gold mirrors and crystal chandeliers. "This will do," she said.

"If we're having our reception in the ballroom, I'd really better learn how to dance," Jack joked, shuffling his paws nervously.

"Well, Dotty doesn't have time to teach you," said Duchess Coco, taking out a long list. "We have far too much to do and must be on our way."

"Will you come with us?" Dotty asked Rosie.

"Bridesmaid at your service!" said Rosie, saluting with her paw. "Maybe Cleo should come, too. She's got great taste."

"Er, sorry," Cleo said. "I'm, um, busy."

That's odd, thought Rosie. Normally Cleo loved to help.

Queen Fifi called for Chester, and a moment later the pony trotted up, pulling the royal carriage. Rosie, Dotty, and the duchess climbed into the plush velvet seats and set off to the center of Petrovia.

Their first stop was Bellissima Bridal Boutique. It was a fancy shop, with beautiful veils hanging from the rails. The shop assistant, a sleek Persian cat, hurried over to wait on them.

"Everyone is delighted about the royal wedding," she gushed. "Whatever Lady Dotty wears is sure to set a fashion trend."

The cat brought out a selection of veils for Dotty to try on. Dotty put on the first veil, which had pretty white polka dots embroidered on it.

"You look gorgeous!" said Rosie, admiring her cousin.

"I love it," said Dotty.

"Too short," said Duchess Coco, shaking her head.

Next Dotty tried on a long beaded veil that trailed several feet behind her when she walked.

"Not bad," said Duchess Coco. "But we

want something really unique. This is a royal wedding, after all."

"Perhaps something from our vintage section," suggested the shop assistant. She brought out an antique veil made of cream-colored lace. "It was worn by Queen Beatrice the Second on her wedding day."

The shop assistant placed the veil over Dotty's head, drowning her in a sea of frilly lace. Rosie thought it made her cousin look like a cross between a ghost and a doily.

"Perfect!" exclaimed Duchess Coco. "This is the one!"

Next they went into Bun-Bun's Bakery to sample wedding cakes. A rabbit in a white

apron was icing a tray of cupcakes with chocolate drops.

"These are special Dotty cupcakes to celebrate the royal wedding," said the baker.

The first cake they tasted was a simple vanilla sponge cake.

"This is really yummy," said Dotty, brushing crumbs off her whiskers. "Vanilla's my favorite flavor."

Rosie nodded, her mouth too full of cake for her to reply.

"No, no, no," said Duchess Coco, pushing her plate away. "This is much too plain."

"Perhaps you would prefer my signature carrot cake?" said the baker, bringing them each a slice of carrot cake to sample.

Rosie took a bite. It was sweet and moist.

"Carrots are too common," said Duchess Coco, wrinkling her nose.

The baker brought them one more cake to try. It had five layers and was covered in swirls of icing and flowers made of edible gold. It was the fanciest cake Rosie had ever seen!

Her belly full, Rosie could only manage one bite. The cake was very rich. Dotty looked a bit queasy.

"Delicious!" cried Duchess Coco. "This will be Dotty's wedding cake."

Their last stop was a florist's shop called Blossoms and Blooms. A parakeet with green feathers was busy arranging a bouquet of pink and white carnations.

"Oh, Lady Dotty," she trilled. "Your wedding is so exciting. My village is having a street party to celebrate."

"Really?" said Dotty.

"Yes, it's going to be a very special day," said Duchess Coco. "So Dotty needs a very special bouquet."

"Let me see," said the parakeet florist. "How about bluebells? They're in season." She brought Dotty a bunch of delicate blue flowers shaped like bells.

"These smell wonderful," said Dotty, burying her nose in the flowers to inhale their sweet scent. "And blue is my favorite color."

Duchess Coco waved the bluebells away.

"Wildflowers aren't suitable for a royal wedding."

Next the florist showed them a pretty bouquet with lilies and orchids.

"Hmmm," said Duchess Coco, unconvinced. "Don't you have anything more exotic?"

The florist brought out an elaborate bouquet of blue roses tied up with a huge silk ribbon. "These are very rare and expensive," she said. "We have to import them from far away."

"Yes!" exclaimed Duchess Coco. "Dotty will carry blue roses—lots and lots of them."

"Do we need to get anything else, Mother?" Dotty asked Duchess Coco.

"No," said the duchess, ticking *flowers* off her list. "That's everything."

Phew! thought Rosie. Planning a wedding was exhausting!

They climbed back into the royal carriage. As Chester trotted to the palace, Rosie spotted a banner hanging in the town square. "Look!" she cried, pointing her paw at the banner.

"'Congratulations, Lady Dotty and Jack!'" Dotty read aloud. She swallowed nervously. "I had no idea my wedding was such a big deal."

"I know!" said Rosie, squeezing her cousin's paw. "Isn't it so exciting?"

Chapter 3

The Bridal Shower

As the wedding drew nearer, Rosie's brides-maid duties kept her very busy. There were musicians to choose, party favors to select, and a menu to plan. Rosie helped Dotty send out hundreds of wedding invitations. Her tongue dried out from licking so many envelopes!

"The Earl of Labrador will sit next to Lady Basset," said Duchess Coco, making final adjustments to the seating plan. "And we'll move Great-Aunt Trixie to table nine."

"Why did we have to invite the Earl of Labrador?" grumbled Dotty. "Or Lady Basset? I barely know them."

"This is a royal wedding," Duchess Coco reminded Dotty, "so we invited all of the kingdom's most important residents."

"I just want to celebrate with my friends and family," Dotty whispered to Rosie.

"Don't worry," said Rosie, grinning. "Your shower is going to be lots of fun."

Rosie had been planning Dotty's bridal shower for days. She wanted it to be perfect. She'd invited all Dotty's friends and asked Petal, the palace cook, to make her cousin's favorite treats. It was going to be amazing!

"Close your eyes," Rosie told Dotty. She led her into the parlor. "Ta-da!"

"Oh, wow!" said Dotty, opening her eyes and gazing at the decorations in awe. Rosie had printed out a huge poster of Jack and Dotty—the same picture her cousin had in her bedroom. There were polka-dot balloons floating in the air and garlands of flowers draped across the room. A table set with a polka-dot tablecloth was piled with delicious-looking food, including the special Dotty cupcakes from Bun-Bun's Bakery. Bella Fierce's song "True Love" was playing softly in the background, and all Dotty's friends were there.

Rosie searched the room for Cleo. Her best friend had been invited to the shower, but she hadn't come. Rosie sighed, feeling guilty. She'd been so busy helping Dotty with her wedding that she hadn't spent much time with Cleo lately. She hoped her friend wasn't upset . . .

"This is very casual," said Duchess Coco, sitting down next to the queen. From the sniffy look on her aunt's face, Rosie guessed that she didn't approve.

Everyone munched dainty roast beef sandwiches and little heart-shaped cheese tarts. Then a guinea pig in a chef's hat bustled into the room, carrying a tray of cookies shaped like wedding bells.

"Everything is delicious, Petal," Rosie told the cook.

"Mmm-hmm," agreed Dotty, helping herself to another cookie.

As they enjoyed the refreshments, one of Dotty's friends asked, "How did you and Jack meet?"

"Oh, it was very romantic," Dotty said. "I was out shopping and it suddenly began to pour with rain. Jack shared his umbrella and walked me all the way home."

"Aww!" cooed the guests.

"How did you meet King Charles, Auntie?" Dotty asked the queen.

Rosie turned to her mother with interest. She'd never heard the story of how her parents had met. She supposed that they had been introduced at a stuffy royal function.

Queen Fifi chuckled. "We met at a disco," she said. "I sneaked out after my bedtime. Prince Charles, as he was back then, was there without his crown. We danced together the whole night, and I didn't realize he was the prince until he invited me to the palace the next day."

Rosie gawked at her mother. She wasn't sure what was more surprising: the idea of her dad dancing all night long or her mom breaking the rules!

Duchess Coco sniffed. "I'm not sure that sets a good example for these youngsters, Fifi. The way the duke and I met was very proper: We sat next to each other at a wedding."

"I remember," said Queen Fifi. "It was *my* wedding!" The queen smiled at Dotty. "I hope you and Jack will be as happy together as King Charles and I have been all these years."

"Hear! Hear!" cried one of Dotty's friends, raising her teacup in a toast.

"We need to make sure that you and Jack have good luck on your wedding day," said Queen Fifi playfully. "Do you have some-thing old, something new, something borrowed, and something blue?"

"That's just a silly superstition," scoffed Duchess Coco.

"No, it's fun!" said Dotty. "Let's see . . . my veil is antique, so that's something old."

"Your cake is something new," Rosie piped up.

"And my flowers will be blue," said Dotty.

"That just leaves something borrowed," said Rosie.

"Maybe I can help with that," said Queen Fifi. She took off the diamond collar she was wearing and fastened it around Dotty's neck.

"Oh, Auntie!" cried Dotty. "It's beautiful, but it's much too valuable."

"Nonsense," said Queen Fifi, waving her paw. "I'd be delighted if you borrowed it for your wedding day."

"I've got something for you, too, Dotty," said one of the guests.

"So do I!" said another.

Dotty opened the presents her friends had given her. There was a pretty polka-dot travel bag to take on her honeymoon, a recipe book called *Cooking for Two*, and an album for Dotty's wedding photos.

"I love them all," said Dotty, happier than Rosie had seen her in ages.

"This is from me," said Rosie, handing Dotty a present. It was the new Bella Fierce album, on which Bella had written *Congratulations, Dotty and Jack. Love, Bella.*

"This is amazing!" said Dotty, hugging her cousin.

"You should open your official wedding gifts now," said Duchess Coco. She rang a little silver bell, and Theodore slowly crawled into the room, balancing a huge tower of gifts on his shell.

Duchess Coco gave Dotty a box. "This is from the Earl of Labrador."

Dotty opened the gift and took out an old-fashioned set of water bowls. "Great," she said unenthusiastically, putting them aside.

"And this one is from Lady Basset," said Duchess Coco.

Dotty unwrapped the present. "Oh," she said flatly. "More water bowls."

"You can never have too many water bowls," said Duchess Coco.

Dotty worked her way through the stack of presents from important wedding guests, opening antique vases, crystal bowls, and other expensive knickknacks. Rosie's cousin looked glummer with every present she opened.

"Let's play some games!" said Rosie, wanting to cheer Dotty up. She took out a picture of Dotty and a wedding veil made out of paper. "This one's called Pin the Veil on the Bride." Rosie put a blindfold over Dotty's eyes and spun her around three times. Everyone laughed when Dotty pinned the veil to her bottom!

Next they played Musical Thrones. The guests danced around a row of thrones as the new Bella Fierce album blasted. When the music stopped, the guests scrambled to find a throne to sit on.

"Sorry, Your Majesty," said one of Dotty's friends, quickly darting into the only

throne left and knocking Queen Fifi out of
the game.

Queen Fifi laughed. "That's quite all
right."

"Can you please turn the music on
again?" Rosie asked Duchess Coco, but
Dotty's mother shook her head.

"No more games," said Duchess Coco disapprovingly.

"But I have lots more planned," protested Rosie.

Duchess Coco shook her head again. "Dotty is getting married tomorrow. She shouldn't be yelping and leaping around like a wild dog."

Bursting into tears, Dotty ran out of the parlor.

"Wedding jitters," said Duchess Coco. "It's only natural."

Rosie ran after her cousin. "Wait, Dotty!" she called.

"I'm sorry, Rosie," sobbed Dotty. "I never expected my wedding to become such a big deal. I just need to get away from all the fuss."

"I know somewhere nobody will bother you," said Rosie. She led Dotty down a long corridor and started climbing up a narrow winding staircase.

"Isn't this the Haunted Tower?" Dotty asked nervously.

"Well, yes," said Rosie. "And no. It's called the Haunted Tower, but it isn't haunted. Nobody ever comes up here."

"But I hear music," said Dotty as they neared the top of the staircase.

That's funny, thought Rosie. Dotty was right; a pretty melody was coming from the tower.

"Hello?" Rosie called. There was a scuffling noise, and the music suddenly stopped.

Stepping warily into the room, Rosie looked around. The tower was crammed full of old furniture, rusting suits of armor, and dusty heirlooms. And there, in the middle of it all, stood Cleo!

"I'm so sorry I missed your bridal shower, Dotty," said Cleo. "I was, er, busy."

AAAACCCHOOO!

"Who's that?" asked Dotty suspiciously. The sneeze seemed to have come from behind a threadbare sofa.

"What?" said Cleo. "Oh, it was me. *AAAACCHOOO!*" Cleo sneezed loudly. "Well,

I've got to get going." She hurried out of the tower.

"I should probably go back to my guests, too," said Dotty, sighing. "I don't want to upset my mother more than I already have."

"I'm sure she's not upset with you," said Rosie. "She just wants the wedding to be perfect."

But as they climbed down the steps, Rosie's mind wasn't on the wedding. It was on her best friend. Why was Cleo acting so strangely?

Chapter 4

The Rehearsal

DUM DUM DEE DUM! DUM DUM DEE DUM!

As the wedding march played loudly on an organ, Rosie eagerly trotted down the aisle, holding a bunch of flowers in her paws. She tried to look elegant, but her rapidly wagging tail gave away how excited she was about being a bridesmaid.

"Slower!" Duchess Coco whispered from

a pew. "This is a wedding, not a running race."

Rosie slowed to a crawl, dragging her paws down the aisle.

"Not that slow," said Duchess Coco.

Sighing, Rosie picked up speed. Being a bridesmaid was harder than it looked!

Luckily, that day was only the wedding rehearsal—a practice for the real thing the next day. The chapel on the palace grounds looked beautiful. It was full of flowers, and there were big blue ribbons at the end of every wooden pew.

As she reached the end of the aisle, Rosie turned around to watch Dotty in her long veil. Lace covered Dotty's face and seemed to stretch a mile behind her. Suddenly, Dotty's paw got tangled up in the veil. She tripped and fell on her bottom.

"Dotty!" cried Jack, running over to help his fiancée get back on her paws.

When Dotty finally made it down the aisle, it was time for Jack and Dotty to practice exchanging their vows.

"Do you, Dotty, take Jack to be your husband?" asked the minister, a big black Doberman wearing a white collar.

"I do," Dotty said.

"And do you, Jack, take Dotty to be your wife?" asked the minister.

"I . . . *CHOOO!*" sneezed Jack. *ACHOOO!* Jack sneezed again, then said, "I do." He sniffed. "Sorry—the flowers are giving me hay fever."

Why does Jack's sneeze sound so familiar? thought Dotty.

"You may now exchange rings," said the minister. There was a long pause. The minster coughed loudly and repeated, "YOU MAY NOW EXCHANGE RINGS."

Still nothing happened.

"Where are the ring bearers?" demanded Duchess Coco, looking around the chapel.

"ROCKY! ROLLO!" called Rosie.

The princes had been napping on their pew.

"What?" cried Rocky, raising his head.

"Huh?" said Rollo, looking around sleepily.

Realizing that everyone was waiting for them, they each grabbed a velvet cushion with a gold ring on it and ran to the front of the chapel.

CRASH! The princes collided, dropping their cushions.

PING! The rings fell on the floor and rolled away under the pews.

"Oops!" said Rocky.

"Don't worry—we'll get them back," said Rollo.

The princes crawled around on the floor, their tails sticking up in the air as they searched for the rings.

Dotty and Jack looked amused, but Duchess Coco huffed loudly in annoyance.

"Got 'em!" Rollo cried at last. He and Rocky hurried back to the bride and groom so they could practice slipping the wedding rings onto each other's paws.

At last, the wedding rehearsal was over.

"That was a complete disaster," wailed

Dotty as they headed back to the palace for dinner.

"You know what they say," said King Charles. "A bad wedding rehearsal is good luck for your wedding day."

"Do they?" asked Dotty doubtfully.

"Oh yes," said Queen Fifi. "Everything went wrong at our wedding rehearsal. The king accidentally stepped on my tail, and it hurt so much I could barely walk down the aisle."

The king chuckled. "She'll never let me live that down."

Dotty smiled faintly, but Rosie could tell that her cousin wasn't convinced.

"Don't worry, Dotty," Rosie said as they walked across the palace grounds.

"Nothing's turning out the way I hoped it would," said Dotty sadly.

"Tomorrow everything will go smoothly," said Rosie. "Yours will be the grandest wedding Petrovia has ever seen."

"Congratulations, Lady Dotty," called Hamish, the squirrel gardener, pausing as he raked the lawn. "I'll be cheering you on tomorrow."

Dotty smiled nervously. "I hope I don't let everyone down."

"Don't be silly," said Rosie. "It's going to be perfect."

When they went inside the palace, Rosie found Cleo humming and dancing around the ballroom.

"Hi, Cleo," Rosie said. "What are you doing?"

Startled, Cleo spun around. "Oh," she gasped. "I'm just, er, practicing for tomorrow."

"For the wedding?" asked Dotty.

"No!" Cleo cried quickly. "For the street party in Catnip Corner." Catnip Corner was the village where Cleo lived.

"That sounds so fun," said Dotty wistfully.

"It will be," said Cleo. "There's going to be music, dancing, and lots of yummy food."

Rosie couldn't shake the feeling that Cleo was hiding something. But what? Best friends never kept secrets from each other.

They all went into the dining room and sat around a long wooden table. Petal served a delicious dinner as everyone chatted about the wedding.

Duchess Coco and Queen Fifi were planning their outfits.

"I'm going to wear my sapphire tiara with a matching collar," said Queen Fifi.

"That sounds lovely," said her sister. "I'm going to wear a hat and the ruby collar Great-Aunt Trixie gave me on my wedding day."

"Oh yes, you look great in red," said Queen Fifi.

King Charles was listening to the duke describe his fitness routine.

"A five-mile run is the best way to start the day," said the duke. "And I always do stretches every morning and night."

"I say, old chap," said King Charles, helping himself to another portion of beef, "I'm tired just hearing you talk about all that exercise."

Jack and the princes were trading jokes.

"What kind of dog is best at keeping time?" Rollo asked Jack.

"I don't know," said Jack.

"A watchdog!" Rocky blurted out.

"That's a good one," Jack said, chuckling. "Now I've got one for you: What do you call a dog who loves baths?"

"What?" asked Rollo.

"A shampoodle!" said Jack.

Rollo howled. Rocky laughed so hard milk came out of his nose.

Cleo and Rosie sat next to each other. They had a lot to catch up on.

"Being a bridesmaid is hard," Rosie told Cleo. "First I walked too fast, and then I walked too slow."

"I'm sure you'll be great tomorrow," said Cleo reassuringly.

The only person who didn't seem to be enjoying herself was Dotty. She just pushed her food around her plate.

"Don't you like your dinner, Lady Dotty?" Petal asked.

"Oh yes," said Dotty. "It's very tasty. I'm just not feeling very hungry."

"Wedding nerves," said Petal sympatheti-cally, patting Dotty on the shoulder. "I couldn't eat a bite before my wedding day, either."

"I'll have yours," said Rocky, scooping Dotty's dinner onto his plate.

"Hey! No fair!" said Rollo. "I want seconds, too."

"There's plenty more," said Petal, serving Rollo a second helping. "You boys have a healthy appetite like your father."

After Petal's yummy chocolate mousse for dessert, Queen Fifi told the puppies to go up to bed.

"But it's still early," whined Rosie.

"You have a big day ahead of you," Queen Fifi said firmly. "And you need to take a bath."

Rosie groaned, but she didn't protest. "See you in the morning!" she called.

As she headed to her room, Rosie peeked inside the parlor. The lacy veil and Queen Fifi's diamond collar were laid out, ready for Dotty to wear the next day. There were vases with two big bouquets of blue roses—one for Rosie and one for Dotty. Towering above it all was the wedding cake, with five layers and swirls of golden icing.

Rosie shivered with excitement. She couldn't wait until the morning!

At dawn, Cleo knocked on Rosie's door to wake her up. For once, Rosie didn't fuss as Cleo brushed her curly fur. She wanted to look her best for Dotty's wedding!

"There!" said Cleo, tying a silky blue ribbon in Rosie's curls. "You look beautiful."

They padded downstairs quietly, not wanting to wake everyone up. The parlor door was open.

"Oh no!" cried Rosie, staring in horror.

Dotty's wedding veil was strewn on the ground, covered in muddy footprints. Huge chunks had been eaten out of the wedding cake. The bouquets had been taken out of their vases, and the roses' blue petals had wilted. Worst of all, Queen Fifi's diamond collar was missing!

This was a disaster!

Chapter 5

Wedding Rescue

"Who did this?" wondered Cleo, picking up the muddy veil. "Why would anyone want to spoil Dotty's wedding?"

"I bet those are Rocky and Rollo's footprints!" said Rosie angrily. "They think weddings are silly, so maybe they wanted to get out of being ring bearers."

"But they love Dotty," said Cleo, sweeping up some crumbs from the ruined wedding cake. "I'm sure the princes wouldn't do anything *that* naughty."

"Dad probably ate the cake," said Rosie. King Charles was known to enjoy a midnight snack or two.

"That doesn't explain the flowers or the collar," said Cleo.

Rosie didn't know who was responsible—but she *did* know one thing. "I've got to find replacements. I'm Dotty's bridesmaid, and I need to fix this so her wedding can go ahead."

"I'll help you," said Cleo. "We can do it!"

"Thanks, Cleo," said Rosie. "I can always count on you." She gazed at the mess. "Let's start with the cake . . ."

Rosie and Cleo bounded downstairs to

the kitchen in the palace's basement. Petal and a whole army of cooks were already hard at work, preparing the wedding feast. A bunny in a white apron was stirring a steaming pot of soup while a guinea pig in a chef's hat rolled out dough.

"Good morning, Princess Rosie," said Petal, looking up from the vegetables she was chopping. "Do you want some porridge?"

"No, Petal," said Rosie, shaking her head. "I want a cake."

"That's not a very healthy breakfast," scolded Petal.

"I don't want cake for breakfast," explained Rosie. "Someone ruined Dotty's wedding cake, and she needs a new one."

Petal gasped. "But that's awful! Who would do such a terrible thing?"

"I don't know, Petal," Rosie said, "but I'm going to put it right."

"Oh dear," fretted Petal. "The cooks and I are all busy making food for the wedding feast. We really don't have time to bake a cake."

"Don't worry," said Rosie. "Cleo and I can bake a new cake."

Petal showed Rosie and Cleo a shelf of cookbooks. The girls flipped through them, searching for a recipe.

"Dotty likes vanilla," said Rosie, remembering what her cousin had said at the bakery.

"How about this one?" suggested Cleo,

showing Rosie a recipe for Velvety Vanilla Cake.

"Perfect!" exclaimed Rosie. "Let's get started!"

Rosie found a big bowl, measuring cups, and a wooden spoon while Cleo gathered the ingredients.

"That's everything we need," said Cleo, putting eggs, flour, baking powder, sugar, butter, and vanilla on the counter.

First they mixed up the butter and sugar, creaming it until it was fluffy. Next Rosie poured in a teaspoon of vanilla and then cracked eggs into the mixture.

"What's next?" asked Rosie, wiping gooey egg white off her paws.

Cleo checked the recipe. "We add the flour and baking powder and mix it all up."

The girls took turns stirring the mixture until the batter was smooth. Rosie greased three circular cake pans with butter, and Cleo poured the batter into them.

"Can you please put these in the oven for us?" Rosie asked Petal.

"Of course," said Petal, sliding the cake pans into a hot oven.

As Cleo set the timer, Rosie washed the mixing bowl and measuring cups they'd used. Soon the delicious aroma of vanilla wafted through the kitchen.

"Something smells good," said one of the cooks.

"Can we do anything to help while the cake bakes?" offered Cleo.

"Yes!" said Petal. "You can be our tasters!"

"Try some chowder," said one cook, ladling out two small bowls.

"Yum!" said Rosie. The soup was rich and creamy.

"Have a mini cheese puff," said another cook, giving them each a dainty little pastry.

"Mmmm," said Cleo, brushing crumbs off her whiskers. "This is delicious."

The girls sampled tiny sausages, salmon mousse, and spicy mini meatballs. They were all scrumptious!

"Everything tastes delicious, Petal," Rosie told the head cook, who beamed proudly.

DING! The timer sounded, and Petal took the three cake pans out of the oven. Rosie and Cleo carefully turned the golden-brown cakes out onto a cooling rack.

While they waited for the cakes to cool, Rosie and Cleo made frosting. They sandwiched the three cakes together with sweet strawberry jam, then covered the whole thing with a thick layer of creamy icing. Finally, they spelled out Dotty's and Jack's names in chocolate drops and made a big heart using strawberries.

"That looks beautiful," said Petal. "You can both come and work in my kitchen anytime."

"Thanks, Petal," said Rosie. "But right now we need to go find Dotty some new flowers."

Rosie and Cleo scampered out into the palace gardens. Dew sparkled on the grass in the morning sunshine. The garden looked perfect, without a weed in sight, and Hamish was busy watering the flower beds.

"Top of the morning, Princess," said the squirrel. "What are you doing up so early?"

"I need to find a new bouquet for Dotty," explained Rosie. "Someone took her blue roses out of their vases and they all wilted."

"Why, that's terrible!" said Hamish, putting down his watering can. "What can I do to help?"

"Can you tell us where to find some more blue roses?" asked Rosie.

Hamish shook his head. "I'm afraid blue roses are rather exotic. They don't grow in Petrovia."

"What about some other type of blue flower?" asked Cleo hopefully.

"I picked all of the blue flowers in the garden to decorate the chapel and the ball-room," Hamish said. "But how about a different color? There are plenty of pretty pink roses, or perhaps some bright yellow sunflowers."

"But blue is Dotty's favorite color," said Rosie. "And she needs something blue on her wedding day so that she and Jack have good luck."

"Ah, yes," realized Hamish, nodding. "Something old, something new, something borrowed, and something blue."

Dotty suddenly remembered something

from her visit to the florist's shop. "Where could we find bluebells, Hamish?"

"Hmmm . . ." The squirrel twitched his bushy tail as he thought. "Bluebells are wildflowers, so you'd need to look in the woods. You might find some near Oak Tree Hollow—"

Before Hamish even finished speaking, Rosie and Cleo had set off across the grass.

"Thanks, Hamish," Rosie called over her shoulder.

"Good luck!" the squirrel called back.

"Let's take the secret shortcut," said Rosie. She darted behind a tree and searched for a mossy hollow by the palace wall. Brushing away some leaves, Rosie found the entrance to a tunnel. She had dug the tunnel the day she'd first met Cleo. Rosie had sneaked out of the palace looking for adventure—and ended up meeting her very best friend!

Rosie and Cleo crawled through the damp, dark tunnel on their bellies, emerging in the woods on the other side of the palace wall. Sunlight filtered through the canopy of leaves, making lacy patterns on the undergrowth. The girls dashed through the trees, searching for bluebells.

"I found some!" called Cleo, picking a few bell-shaped blossoms.

Rosie ran into a clearing and bumped right into an old friend. *CRASH!*

"Hi, Princess Rosie," said Charlie, helping her up. "Hi, Cleo."

The squirrel boy was with his parents and his siblings. They each held a basket filled with acorns, walnuts, and hazelnuts.

"We're gathering nuts for the Oak Tree Hollow street party to celebrate the royal wedding," explained Charlie's mother.

"Are you looking for nuts, too, Princess Rosie?" asked Charlie's little sister shyly.

"No," said Rosie. "We're looking for bluebells."

"Someone ruined Lady Dotty's wedding bouquet," explained Cleo, "so we're making her a new one."

"Oh, what a shame," said Charlie's dad.

"We'll help you find bluebells," offered Charlie.

With the help of Charlie and his family, Rosie and Cleo soon had two massive bunches of bluebells.

"Thanks so much for your help," said Rosie.

"No problem," said Charlie. "We're all really happy for Lady Dotty and Jack."

By then the sun had risen higher in the sky. The sound of church bells rang out across the woods.

"Oh no," cried Rosie. "It's already noon!"

They had baked a cake and found blue flowers—but they still needed to find a new veil and collar for Dotty. There was no time to lose!

Chapter 6

Catnip Corner

"Where did Dotty get her wedding veil?" Cleo asked Rosie.

"It was from a shop called Bellissima Bridal Boutique," said Rosie.

"Let's see if we can get another veil there," suggested Cleo.

They ran through the woods until they reached the center of Petrovia. The streets were lined with shops and cafés. The last time Rosie had gone there, in the royal carriage, the streets had been bustling. Today it was very quiet.

"I think it's this way," said Rosie, leading Cleo down a side street.

"There it is!" cried Cleo, spotting the shop's sign.

There were no lights on inside the bridal boutique, and shutters covered the windows.

Rosie pounded on the door. "Open up, please! It's an emergency!"

Nobody answered.

A cat walking her three kittens gave Rosie a strange look. "All the shops are closed today," she said.

"Why?" asked Rosie.

The kittens giggled.

"Where have you been, dear?" the cat asked kindly. "It's so everyone can celebrate the royal wedding, of course!"

Rosie groaned. There wouldn't *be* a royal wedding if she couldn't find a veil for Dotty. "What are we going to do?" she wailed.

Cleo thought for a moment. "Let's go see my mom," she said. "She'll help us."

Rosie and Cleo raced to a village with pretty cottages painted in soft pastel pinks, blues, and yellows. A tabby cat was hanging up decorations in the town square while other cats were setting out long trestle tables. In the bandstand, a band of cat musicians were tuning their instruments.

"Oops!" the tabby cat said as one of his claws accidentally popped a purple balloon.

Cleo knocked on the door of a pale blue cottage with herbs growing in window boxes. Cleo's mother opened the door. She had fluffy gray fur like her daughter and wore a flowery apron. "Hello, dear," she said. "I wasn't expecting you back from the palace so soon." Suddenly noticing Rosie behind Cleo, she curtsied and said, "Welcome, Your Highness."

Rosie and Cleo went into the cottage.

"I was just making food for the street party," said Cleo's mom, showing the girls a towering platter of sandwiches.

"Mmmm, tuna—my favorite," said Cleo, grabbing two for herself and Rosie.

Rosie wolfed the sandwich down in a very unprincessy way. She hadn't eaten anything since they had tasted Petal's wedding food, and she was hungry!

"Can you help us, Mom?" asked Cleo. "Someone ruined Lady Dotty's veil, and we need to find her a new one fast."

"Actually, we don't need a new veil. We need an old one," said Rosie. "Dotty needs something old for good luck."

"Do you still have your wedding veil?" Cleo asked her mother hopefully.

"Hmmm," Cleo's mom said. "I wore your grandmother's wedding veil. Grannie made it herself."

Cleo's mother went to the fireplace and

took down a photograph in a silver frame. "This is me and your father on our wedding day," she said, handing it to Cleo and Rosie.

In the photo, Cleo's mom was holding a bouquet of pink and white tulips and was gazing into her husband's eyes adoringly.

"You look so pretty!" said Rosie.

"Thank you," said Cleo's mom, smiling. "It was one of the happiest days of my life."

Rosie and Cleo exchanged worried looks. They wanted Dotty's wedding day to be filled with joy, too—but time was running out!

"So can Dotty wear the veil?" asked Cleo.

"Of course," said Cleo's mom. "But it's at Grannie's house."

Fortunately, Cleo's grandmother lived

nearby, in a pink cottage a few doors down the street, so Rosie and Cleo went to see her.

"Hello, dear," an elderly gray cat with glasses balanced on her pink nose said as she opened the door. She gave Cleo a kiss. Peering through her spectacles at Rosie, she asked, "And who do we have here?"

"This is my friend Princess Rosie, Grannie," said Cleo.

"Oh my word!" said the old cat. "I'm sorry I didn't recognize you, Your Highness." Balancing on her cane, she started to curtsy.

Rosie stopped her. "That's not necessary. And you can just call me Rosie."

"Grannie, we have a big favor to ask,"

said Cleo. "Can Lady Dotty wear your wedding veil? Someone spoiled hers, and it's nearly time for the wedding."

"It would be an honor," said Grannie. Then she frowned. "Now where on earth is it?"

"We'll help you look," said Cleo.

The girls searched through Grannie's dresser. They didn't find the veil, but they found some baby pictures of Cleo.

"You were so cute!" said Rosie, smiling at a photo of a tiny Cleo with her eyes shut.

Next they checked Grannie's closet. The veil wasn't in there, either, but the girls found a collection of floppy old-fashioned hats.

"Did you really wear these?" Cleo asked

her grandmother, holding up a wide-brimmed hat with a flower on it.

"They were very fashionable back in the day," said Grannie.

Giggling, Cleo and Rosie took turns modeling the hats.

"It might be in here," said Grannie, sliding a wooden chest out from under her bed.

Cleo opened the box's lid. *Creak!*

"Pee-yew!" Cleo said, waving her paw in front of her nose as the smell of mothballs wafted out. There was something wrapped in tissue paper at the bottom of the trunk. Cleo carefully lifted it out and unwrapped layers and layers of tissue.

It was Grannie's wedding veil!

"Oh, wow!" gasped Rosie. Edged in lace and attached to a delicate pearl tiara, the veil was the most beautiful she had ever seen. It wasn't long and fancy like Dotty's ruined veil, but Rosie had a feeling her cousin would like it even more.

"Did you really make this?" Cleo asked her grandmother.

"Oh yes," said Grannie. "I was a seamstress before you were born. I'll show you."

She led the girls to a sewing machine. Next to it was a wicker basket, lined in red gingham. Grannie opened the sewing basket, revealing pins, needles, and spools of thread. There were buttons and beads, a measuring tape, and a shiny silver thimble.

"That's really interesting, Grannie," said Cleo. "But we still need to find a collar for Dotty to wear."

Grannie let the girls rummage through her jewelry box, but there was nothing quite right for Dotty.

"What about this one?" asked Cleo, showing Rosie a small gold collar.

Rosie shook her head. "I don't think that will fit Dotty."

"They'll all be too small, so why don't you make one that's just her size?" said Grannie, holding up her tape measure.

"That's a great idea!" exclaimed Rosie.

"Is there enough time?" Cleo asked, fretting.

"There will be if I help you," said Grannie.

Cleo's grandmother helped the girls measure a length of silky white ribbon and cut it to the right size. They rummaged through the sewing basket and found some pearl beads. Working quickly, the girls stitched the pearls onto the ribbon while Grannie sewed on a delicate clasp. In no time, Dotty's collar was finished.

"Oh no!" said Rosie, suddenly remembering something. "Dotty's collar was her 'something borrowed.' But this collar is brand-new!"

Grannie took a gold heart-shaped brooch out of her jewelry box. "There," she said, pinning it to the middle of the collar. "Dotty can borrow this."

Now the collar looked even lovelier— and was sure to bring Dotty and Jack good luck!

Checking the time on the alarm clock on Grannie's bedside table, Rosie gasped. "We've got to get back to the palace."

"One more thing," said Grannie. She took a spool of pale blue ribbon out of her sewing basket and she snipped off two lengths. Then she tied the ribbons around the two bouquets of bluebells and handed them to the girls.

"Thanks for everything, Grannie!" said Cleo, giving her grandmother a kiss.

"Yes, thank you very much," said Rosie, also giving Grannie a kiss.

Rosie and Cleo hurried back to the palace as fast as they could, carefully holding the veil, the collar, and the two bouquets.

"We'll have to go through the front gates," said Rosie. "Dotty's veil would get dirty if we went through the secret tunnel."

A big crowd was gathered outside the palace's golden gates. Everyone was cheering and calling Dotty's and Jack's names.

"They're hoping to catch a glimpse of the happy couple," Cleo said.

"They'll be out of luck unless we can get in," said Rosie, diving into the crowd.

"Coming through," she yelled, holding the veil above her head.

"Excuse me," said Cleo, trying to protect the flowers as she squeezed past.

Finally, they made it to the front of the crowd. A bulldog in a purple-and-gold uniform was guarding the gates.

"No entry," he barked.

"It's me, Winston," said Rosie. "Princess Rosie."

"Sorry, Your Highness," said the guard dog, opening the gates. "I didn't realize you'd gone out."

"Hang on, Dotty!" cried Rosie as she sprinted across the palace lawn. "We're coming!"

Chapter 7

Runaway Bride

"We're back!" Rosie cried, bursting into the parlor.

King Charles and Queen Fifi were consoling a sobbing Duchess Coco.

"Don't worry," said Rosie. "We fixed everything. Cleo's grandmother loaned us her wedding veil, we made Dotty a collar, and we picked two bouquets of bluebells." She held up the veil in one paw and a bunch of flowers in the other.

"And we baked a new wedding cake," added Cleo, who was holding the collar and the second bouquet.

"So Dotty has everything she needs for her wedding," Rosie announced.

For some reason, that made Duchess Coco cry even louder.

The duke was pacing around the room. Even Rocky and Rollo looked solemn.

"Wait . . ." Rosie said, looking around the room. "Where's Dotty?"

"That's just it," said Rollo. "Nobody knows."

"She's vanished," said Rocky.

"WAAHHH!" sobbed the duchess.

"There, there," said Queen Fifi, patting

her sister on the head. "I'm sure she'll turn up soon."

"But the wedding is about to start," wailed Duchess Coco. "Jack will be waiting for Dotty at the altar."

There was a knock on the parlor door. "The detective has arrived, Your Majesty," said Theodore.

"Show him in, please," King Charles told the tortoise butler.

Theodore crawled off and returned with a bloodhound wearing a deerstalker hat. The dog was holding a magnifying glass in his paw.

"I'm Inspector Bailey," said the detective in a gruff voice. "What seems to be the problem?"

"Thank you for coming," said King Charles. "It's my niece, Lady Dotty. She's—"

"MISSING!" wailed Duchess Coco, bursting into fresh floods of tears.

"Hmmm," said the bloodhound. Peering through the magnifying glass with his sad-looking eyes, he circled the room slowly. He paused to examine the wedding veil, the collar, and the bouquets of flowers. "From the clues I have found, I deduce that there is going to be a wedding."

Rocky and Rollo rolled their eyes.

"You don't need to be a detective to figure that out," Rocky whispered.

"It's Dotty's wedding day," explained Queen Fifi. "She's supposed to be getting married to Jack, but she's nowhere to be found."

"Aha!" exclaimed Inspector Bailey. "I have a hunch that she does not wish to marry this Jack. She has run away to avoid her wedding."

"I don't think so," said the duke, shaking his head. "They are very much in love."

Everyone nodded in agreement.

"This is my Dotty," said Duchess Coco, showing the detective a photograph of Dotty and Jack.

"Which one is Dotty?" asked the detective, studying the photograph.

"Er, Dotty is the spotty one," said the duchess.

"They do look very happy," said the detective. "Maybe they ran away together."

"No," said Queen Fifi. "I checked Dotty's room. Nothing was missing."

"Does anyone else have a theory?" asked the detective.

"Maybe she was dognapped!" said Rocky.

That set Duchess Coco off again. Queen Fifi glared at Rocky and stroked her sister's fur soothingly.

"Have you received a ransom note?" inquired Inspector Bailey.

"No," said the duke. "Just lots of wedding cards."

Inspector Bailey took a card with a picture of a wedding cake on it from a big pile. He examined it with his magnifying glass.

"That's from Great-Aunt Trixie," said Queen Fifi. "I don't think it's suspicious."

"A detective doesn't overlook any clues," the bloodhound said.

"Maybe we should organize a search party?" suggested King Charles.

"An excellent suggestion," said Inspector Bailey. "Are you by any chance a trained police officer?"

"Er, no," said Rosie's dad. "I'm the king."

Inspector Bailey eyed King Charles suspiciously, as if he didn't believe him.

"King Charles II?" said the king. "I'm the king of Petrovia . . ."

Rosie looked at Cleo despairingly. Inspector Bailey didn't have a clue—and not just about where Dotty could be!

"Right," said King Charles, taking command. "Let's split up so we can cover more ground. Rocky and Rollo will come with me."

The princes high-fived with their paws.

"The duke can go with Inspector Bailey," continued the king. He turned to Cleo and Rosie. "You two always make a good team, so you should stick together."

Rosie and Cleo nodded.

"I'll stay here with the duchess," said Queen Fifi.

"Don't worry," Inspector Bailey told her. "We'll soon sniff Dopey out."

"DOTTY!" Rosie said, correcting him.

"No, thank you," said Inspector Bailey. "I don't need to use the potty. I went before I left the police station."

Rocky and Rollo tried—and failed—to stifle their giggles.

"Let's get going!" said King Charles, hurrying the princes out of the parlor.

"Where should we look for Dotty first?" Cleo asked Rosie.

Rosie thought hard. The palace was full of hiding places.

"Let's try the kitchen," Rosie said.

Unaware that Dotty was missing, Petal and the other cooks were putting the finishing touches on the wedding feast.

The wedding cake Rosie and Cleo had baked was resting on a fancy china cake stand.

"Have you seen Dotty anywhere?" Rosie asked, peering under a wooden table while Cleo searched the pantry.

"No," said Petal. "She hasn't been down here."

"Maybe she's outside," said Cleo.

Rosie and Cleo went into the garden and checked inside Hamish's toolshed. Rocky and Rollo liked to hide in there sometimes, but there was no sign of Dotty.

"Did you find some bluebells?" Hamish asked them, walking into the shed to put away his watering can.

"Yes, we did," said Rosie. *It's just Dotty we can't find now!* she thought.

"Maybe she's hiding under one of the beds," suggested Cleo.

Rosie gulped. There were a lot of beds in the palace!

"Let's start with my room," said Rosie.

They rushed back inside and up the stairs, past Priscilla, who was dusting picture frames.

"Princesses should NEVER run," scolded the housekeeper. "They should ALWAYS walk."

Rosie ignored Priscilla, taking the stairs two at a time.

In her bedroom, Rosie lifted her pink

satin bedspread and checked under the bed. Crawling on her tummy, she found a dusty collar and a tennis ball, but no Dotty.

"Hey, Rosie," called Cleo. "Have you seen this?"

Wriggling out from under the bed, Rosie got back on her feet. Cleo was holding a note.

Rosie read it out loud:

Dear Rosie,

   I'm sorry, but I needed to get away. I went where nobody will find me.

Love,

Dotty

Suddenly, Rosie knew exactly where her cousin was hiding.

"The Haunted Tower!" she cried, wagging her tail. "Dotty's in the Haunted Tower!"

Rosie skittered down the hallway with Cleo following. She bounded up the stairs of the tower, her curly ears flapping. She desperately hoped that she was right!

Bursting into the room, she saw her cousin gazing out a narrow window.

"Dotty!" she panted.

As Dotty turned to face her, Rosie saw that her cousin's eyes were filled with tears. She was holding Queen Fifi's collar.

"Don't cry, Dotty!" said Rosie, rushing over to hug her. "Your wedding is going to be fine. We baked you a cake, found blue flowers, borrowed a veil, and made you a collar. I don't know who did such a terrible thing, but Cleo and I fixed everything."

That just made Dotty cry even harder.

"What's wrong?" Rosie asked. "Please don't cry. We'll find whoever did this."

"I already know who did it, Rosie," Dotty sobbed, covering her face with her paws. "It was ME!"

Chapter 8

Street Party!

Rosie and Cleo stared at Dotty. They couldn't believe what they had just heard. Dotty had destroyed her own wedding. It didn't make any sense!

"But why?" asked Rosie. "Why would you do that?"

"Don't you want to marry Jack?" asked Cleo.

"Yes!" cried Dotty. "I love Jack! I do want to marry him."

"So what's the problem?" asked Rosie, still confused.

"I never wanted a fancy royal wedding and all this attention," explained Dotty. She curled up on an old sofa with stuffing coming out of its cushions. "Look at all the people outside the palace gates. I know I should feel honored, but all this fuss makes me really uncomfortable."

"Why didn't you say anything before?" asked Rosie.

"Because I didn't want to disappoint my mom," said Dotty. "She loved the idea of a grand royal wedding that everyone in Petrovia would be talking about."

"But it's *your* wedding," said Rosie.

"It should be about what *you* *and* *Jack* want."

Cleo nodded. "What *do* you want, Dotty?"

Brushing a tear away with her paw, Dotty sniffed. "I just wanted a fun party where Jack and I could dance, have fun with our friends and family, and eat yummy food. I don't care about impressing everyone in Petrovia."

Rosie went to the window and looked out. In the distance, she could see the purple and gold balloons in Catnip Corner bobbing in the breeze. The faint sound of music from the street party carried across the palace grounds.

"Maybe you can still have that . . ." said

Rosie. Her tail wagged quickly, the way it always did when she had a good idea!

"What do you mean?" asked Dotty.

"I'll explain later," said Rosie. "First we've got to tell everyone that we found you. Your parents are really worried."

"Everyone's going to be so annoyed with me," Dotty said, worried, as they headed downstairs.

"No, they're not," Cleo assured her. "They're just going to be relieved to see you."

The other search teams had gathered back in the parlor.

"We checked the gardens and the greenhouses," said King Charles.

"We searched the ballroom and the banquet hall," said the duke.

"We looked in the Haunted Tower," said Rosie, leading Dotty into the parlor, "and look who we found . . ."

"Dotty!" cried Duchess Coco, running over to hug her daughter.

Inspector Bailey looked from Dotty to the photo in his paw. Holding his magnifying glass to his droopy eyes, he inspected Dotty. "Aha!" he announced triumphantly. "I have tracked down the missing bride!"

"No, you didn't," said Cleo. "Rosie found her."

"Case closed," said the bloodhound. "So I will be on my way." He patted Rosie on the head. "Excellent detective work, young pup. You'd make a fine sleuth."

"Thanks," said Rosie. "But I'm happy being a princess."

"I'm sorry I ran away," said Dotty, tears misting her eyes. "I just felt overwhelmed by all of this." She handed Queen Fifi her diamond collar.

"No, *I'm* sorry," said Duchess Coco. "I got carried away. I didn't listen to what you wanted."

The duke nodded. "This should have been the wedding of your dreams."

"It still can be," said Rosie, "if Dotty gets ready quickly."

"I'll run over to the chapel and get Jack,"

said the duke. "I'm sure he's wondering where everyone is."

"Get the minister, too!" called Rosie as the duke sprinted off.

Duchess Coco and Queen Fifi helped Dotty get dressed. Duchess Coco placed the pearl tiara on Dotty's head while the queen arranged the filmy white veil around her.

"This is so beautiful," said Dotty.

"My grannie sewed it," Cleo said proudly.

"Do you want to wear my mom's diamond collar?" Rosie asked Dotty.

"If it's okay with you, Queen Fifi, could I wear the one Rosie and Cleo made for me?" asked Dotty.

"Of course," said the queen, smiling.

Rosie and Cleo clasped the collar around Dotty's neck.

"It's lovely," said Dotty, admiring the heart-shaped brooch.

"And so are you," said Rosie.

"Don't forget these," said Cleo, handing Dotty and Rosie their bouquets of bluebells.

"Thanks for your help, Cleo. Would you like to be my flower girl?" Dotty asked.

"I'd love that!" purred Cleo, beaming.

Cleo gathered up all the petals that had fallen off the blue roses and put them into a basket while Rosie went to get Petal and the wedding cake.

They returned at the same time as Jack, the duke, and the minister.

"Oh, wow!" gasped Jack, staring at his bride.

Dotty looked stunning.

King Charles called for the royal carriage, and few moments later, Chester clip-clopped up the path.

"Where to, Your Majesty?" Chester asked.

"Rosie?" the king asked.

"To Catnip Corner, please," said Rosie, holding Dotty's veil so her cousin could climb into the carriage.

It was a tight squeeze in the carriage, but the whole family managed to fit inside. As they rolled through the palace gates, the crowd gave a big cheer. Dotty and Jack waved happily to their well-wishers.

Another carriage, with all their friends from the palace, followed them. Theodore balanced the wedding cake on his shell; Hamish had his bagpipes; and Petal and Priscilla each held one of the pageboys' cushions.

When they got to Catnip Corner, Jack and the minister took their places on the bandstand. As Hamish played a wedding march on his bagpipes, Cleo sprinkled blue rose petals along the path.

"Are you ready, Dotty?" Rosie asked her cousin.

Dotty nodded and smiled. "I am now."

DUM DUM DEE DUM!

Holding her bluebell bouquet in her

paws, Rosie walked down the path to the bandstand. Then she watched the Duke of Dalmatia proudly walk his daughter down the aisle. Even though the veil was covering Dotty's face, Rosie could tell that her cousin was smiling.

"Do you, Dotty, take Jack to be your husband?" asked the minister.

"I do," said Dotty, her voice ringing out loud and clear.

"And do you, Jack, take Dotty to be your wife?" asked the minister.

"I do," said Jack.

"You may kiss the bride!" declared the minister.

Jack lifted Dotty's veil and gave her a big kiss.

"Yay!" cheered the crowd.

"WAH!" sobbed Duchess Coco, this time crying tears of joy!

As wedding bells rang out, Dotty and Jack cut their wedding cake. Cleo and Rosie handed slices to all the guests.

"Mmmm. This is delicious," said Jack.

"Vanilla is my favorite," said Dotty, nibbling her piece happily.

A band of cat musicians started to play Bella Fierce's hit song "True Love."

"Shall we?" Jack asked, bowing to Dotty. Then, taking his bride's paw, he twirled her

around the town square. He and Dotty danced together gracefully, gliding in time to the music.

"Wow!" said Rosie, impressed. "I thought Jack wasn't a good dancer, but he's amazing!"

"He's been having lessons," said Cleo, giggling. "From me!"

So that *was Cleo's secret,* thought Rosie. That was why her friend had been acting strange!

"I hated hiding it from you," Cleo confessed. "But Jack wanted it to be a surprise. You almost caught us practicing in the Haunted Tower."

Aha! thought Rosie. That was why Jack's sneeze sounded so familiar!

After the happy couple had finished their first dance, it was time for everyone to join in!

Holding paws, Rosie and Cleo danced to every song. Hamish did a merry jig; Priscilla shook her fluffy tail; and even Theodore nodded his head to the beat!

"Look at Mom and Dad!" Rocky said, giggling.

The king spun the queen around, then lowered her into a dip.

"That's so embarrassing!" said Rollo, covering his face with his paw.

Harris County Public Library, Houston, TX

Rosie thought her parents looked cute. "That's how they met, you know," she told her brothers.

The afternoon flew by in a blur of music, dancing, and tasty treats. Soon it was time for Jack and Dotty to leave for their honeymoon.

"Thank you so much for everything, Rosie," said Dotty, hugging her cousin. "You've been the best bridesmaid ever."

"And you've been an amazing flower girl—and dance teacher," Jack said, grinning at Cleo.

Jack and Dotty climbed into the royal carriage and waved good-bye.

"Good luck!" everyone cried.

Harris County Public Library, Houston, TX

But Rosie knew they didn't need luck. They had something even more important—love.

As the carriage pulled away, Dotty threw her wedding bouquet into the crowd.

Priscilla jumped up and caught it!

"You know what that means, Priscilla," said King Charles, chuckling. "You'll be getting married next."

The rabbit giggled and buried her nose in the bluebells.

Rosie grinned. She hoped that there *would* be another wedding at Pawstone Palace soon. Being a bridesmaid was the best!

5